First published 2012 Parragon Books, Ltd.

Copyright © 2018 Cottage Door Press, LLC
5005 Newport Drive, Rolling Meadows, Illinois 60008
All Rights Reserved

10 9 8 7 6 5 4 3 2 1

ISBN: 978-1-68052-447-5

Parragon Books is an imprint of Cottage Door Press, LLC.
Parragon Books® and the Parragon® logo are registered trademarks of Cottage Door Press, LLC.

Goldilocks
and the
Three Bears

Retold by Sarah Delmege
Illustrated by Gavin Scott

Once upon a time, Goldilocks was playing in the woods near her home.

As she skipped along the pebbly path, her golden locks bouncing, Goldilocks suddenly stopped and sniffed the air …

A yummy smell was coming from the middle of the woods.

RUMBLE, RUMBLE!

As her tummy grumbled loudly, Goldilocks followed the delicious smell. She soon found herself in front of a little house.

"I wonder who lives here ... " she said.

Goldilocks knocked loudly on the front door.

KNOCK, KNOCK, KNO ...

But on the last KNOCK, the door swung open.
There was no one at home.

Goldilocks saw three bowls of porridge on the
kitchen table.

"I'm sure no one will mind if
I have a little taste of this porridge,"
she told herself.

Goldilocks ate a spoonful
of porridge from the
biggest bowl.

"Yuck!" she cried.
"This porridge
is much too cold!"

Goldilocks tried the
medium-size bowl.

"Ouch!" she gasped.
"This porridge is much
too hot!"

Finally, Goldilocks took a little mouthful from the smallest bowl.

"Mmmm!" she sighed. "This porridge is perfect!"

And she ate it all up.

Then, Goldilocks went into the living room for a rest. She saw a big chair, a medium-size chair, and a tiny, little chair.

Goldilocks climbed onto the biggest chair.

"This chair is too big!" she said.

Next, Goldilocks clambered onto the medium-size chair.
The cushions were very squishy.

"This chair is too soft!" she cried.

Then, Goldilocks tried the tiny chair.

"This chair is perfect!" beamed Goldilocks.
She was just getting comfortable, when ...

CR-R-R-RACK!

The chair broke into pieces.

"Oh, no!" Goldilocks gasped.
"Perhaps I should lie down instead."

Upstairs, Goldilocks found
a big bed, a medium-size bed,
and a tiny, little bed.

When she jumped on the
big bed it was too hard. The
medium-size bed was too soft
for bouncing, and the little
bed was …

"Perfect!" Goldilocks sighed
happily.

And the little girl crawled
under the covers and fell
fast asleep.

ZzzzzzZZZzzzzzz

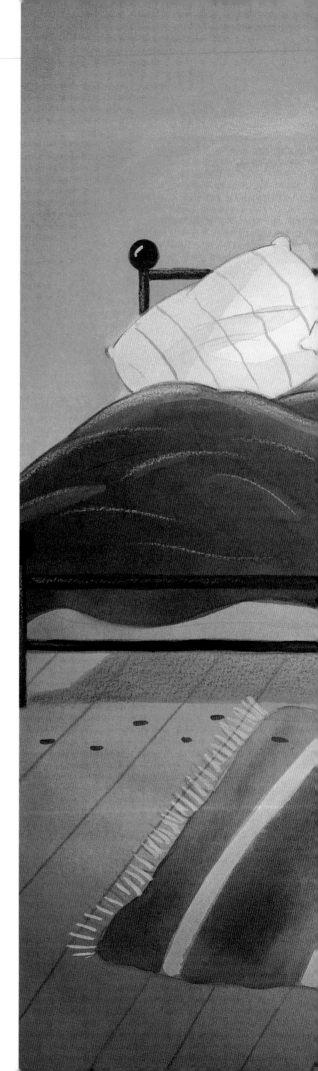

Meanwhile, three hungry bears returned
to the little house. They had been for a
walk while their hot porridge cooled down.

But the door was already open, and there
were muddy footprints in the hall …

"Someone's been eating my porridge!" roared Daddy Bear.

ROAR!

"Someone's been eating my porridge too," growled Mommy Bear.

"Look!" squeaked Baby Bear. "My porridge has all gone!"

The three bears went into the living room.

"Someone's been sitting in my chair!" roared Daddy Bear.

"Someone's been sitting in my chair too," growled Mommy Bear.

"Someone's been sitting in my chair," squeaked Baby Bear, "and they've broken it!"

Suddenly, the three bears heard a noise coming from upstairs ...

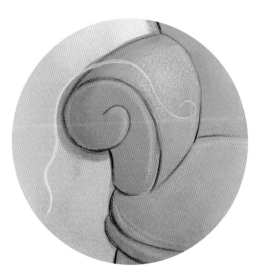

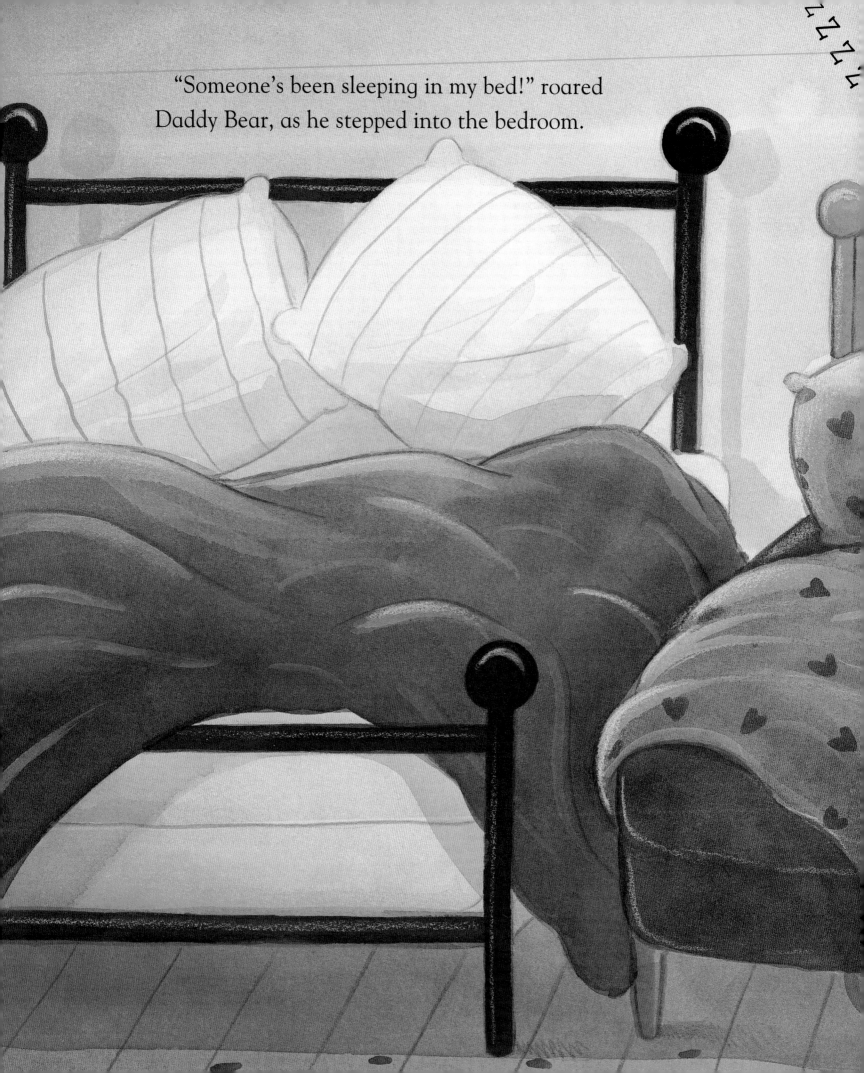

"Someone's been sleeping in my bed!" roared
Daddy Bear, as he stepped into the bedroom.

"Someone's been sleeping in my bed too," growled Mommy Bear, straightening the cover.

ZZZZZZZZZZZZZZZZZZZZZZZ

"Someone's been sleeping in my bed," squeaked Baby Bear, "and she's still there!"

Goldilocks woke up with a start and screamed.

The three bears watched in surprise as she ran off through the forest as fast as her little legs would carry her.

And guess what? The three bears never saw Goldilocks again.

The End